A Battleaxe and a Metal Arm 1:

Death without Direction

Samuel Fleming

Thank you to my Beta Readers

and to my First Reader,

Mel.

iv

Contents

"Death is not the end."

—*nameless*

Born without Memory

The first thing Helesys knew was falling.

It was long enough for her heart to rise into her throat and thankfully no longer than that. She landed on both feet and crouched into a roll to spare her legs. Twice over and then sprawled out on the dusty stone floor.

The elf pushed to her feet quickly because a short step away someone else fell to the ground. He did not land as graceful but he did not need to. The man hit the ground in a crouch, catching himself through sheer strength alone. He stood easily and relaxed, finally towering shoulders above Helesys. He wore thick leather armor. A fur cloak and battleaxe sat across his shoulders, making him look like a mountain in the sharp light of the room.

His voice was cold as stone. "Who are you?"

Helesys measured the man and took him for an outlander, a barbarian nomad. Savages to some… but not to her.

This gave her pause. She sensed this man was not a danger to her, but she did not know how she knew. Helesys searched her memories and found more shroud, more void.

"Are you mute?"

"Give me silence a moment," she replied sternly.

He grunted in response, but stood still and waited.

Helesys looked around the room. It was three stories high and barely the same across. They were clearly underground—the room was sparsely lit by threads of light from above and sconces that burned along the wall. This fact alone did not bother her, as her eyes did well enough in the dim. All around, the room was made of wide stone blocks. They were pitted and rough in spots and covered by green-red moss in others.

Wherever they were, it was ancient and worn. The air was stale and still.

No, the thing that troubled Helesys was that could remember scarcely more than her name. She knew things… but could not remember the context. She could discern things about the underground room, but could not remember where she was or why she was in this place.

Worse was that she could not see an opening above them. No telling how they got in or how they might get back out.

"My name is Helesys," she finally said while scanning the room. "I do not remember more than that." It was a half-truth. Her family name was Byyra.

"My name is Taunauk. My memory has been stolen as well," he replied. "I know *what* I am, but I have forgotten *who*."

"I do not follow."

"I am from the forest and the fields and the mountains. I am human. I am a warrior." He pulled the giant axe overhead and held it firmly. It was taller than Helesys and nearly as tall as the barbarian. It had twin blades on the head, razor sharp yet chipped at the points and the rest of the metal was dulled with wear. The leather wrap of the handle was worn pale at the grips.

"I know this axe," he said. "It echoes in my hands but I cannot sense its origin."

Helesys looked herself over as the human talked. She was an elf, tall (compared to *most* humans) and slender. White hair draped over her shoulder. Beneath her grey robes she felt the silken weight of elven chainmail, of mithral. Her hands and skin were noble-fair, but she felt strong and poised—which had helped her landing and tumble—

—Her right arm had felt like it was covered in a gauntlet beneath her sleeve. The metal was a bright silver with a hue of blue—the same mithral as her chainmail—but it was more: Her entire right arm was metal prosthetic from fingertip to shoulder. No skin or muscle or bone remained—yet it was as dexterous as her left hand. She looked at her arm with wonder for she could feel the supple weight and fabric of her robe upon the metal surface.

And in her forearm, embedded deep within the length of metal where a bone ought to be, was a magic wand. She knew this—felt this—because the wand wasn't just hidden inside her arm, but connected to her arm. So she was a mage. A spellslinger.

But again her memory was a void. Helesys couldn't remember when or how she had gotten her arm. She couldn't remember her spells or her training or her teacher.

"Are you a weaver?" Taunauk asked, bringing her back to the tomb. "You have that look about you. Noble, fair-skinned. Cunning." He said the words plainly and without disdain. That surprised her. If anything, there was confusion in his voice, as if the term *weaver* was familiar but disconnected. He did not mention her arm.

"I believe so. I know so… As you said, I know what I am, but I have forgotten who." Helesys looked around the room and saw a passageway—a single passageway. "Since there seems to be no other exit, are you against traveling together?"

"I am not," the barbarian replied. He walked over to the closest sconce and with a smooth pull he ripped it from the wall, sending bits of stone scattering across the floor. The quiet display of strength contrasted with the breaking of the attachment and scattering of stone fragments across the floor.

In the flickering torchlight, his face was rough with creases, and his hair and beard were cut to nothing but stubble.

"I will go first." Taunauk said. He led the way with torch in one hand and battleaxe in the other.

Helesys offered no counterpoint and followed the hulk of a man. Meanwhile she flexed the fingers of her mechanical hand. Inside the arcane gears spun and pistons pulsed with oily silence. She felt the flow of power from the wand within, like bottled lightning.

Confidence burned within her and somehow she knew that she should feel sorry for any denizens of the underground that crossed her and Taunauk. The two of them could not have been more different, yet they were forced by circumstance to work together. Helesys wondered if they had known each other before they dropped into this place.

But it was an impossible question—one quickly replaced with the silence of the hallway.

~

Cold stone surrounded them as Taunauk led the way down the hall. The hallway was robust, nearly ten paces wide and just as tall, but with the barbarian for reference it felt cramped. Helesys only understood its size when she reached out with both hands and could not touch either wall.

The hallway stretched on straight with no deviation or change for half a mile, until they came to an opening. At first it looked as if the entire hallway disappeared into a black void, but as they approached they could see that the hallway merely stopped for a while and started again some twenty feet away.

Taunauk crouched lower as he approached, impossibly silent, like a giant cat stalking prey. Helesys followed, matching his cadence. Slowly he peered around the corner, looking both ways, and waved for her to approach.

Helesys stepped beside him and peered out across the chasm. The space between had been hollowed out into a gigantic cylinder that cut perpendicular to the hallway like an underground river had once cut across it. A hundred yards away in either direction the hollow of the river had collapsed, such that the only choice forward was down into the dry riverbed and directly across it to the counterpart hallway.

Taunauk grasped the torch with two spare fingers of his axehand, somehow holding the massive weapon and the torch in the same hand. Then reached around the edge of the stone and brought back a clump of surrounding dirt. He rubbed it together and it fell away in dry powder.

"Dry soil. Old passage," he whispered. He slid down from the hallway to the dirt floor of the cylinder in swift silence. "Safe."

Helesys followed. It was an easy enough drop but she could not quite match the barbarian's cat-like grace. She knew from that point on it would be a personal challenge for herself.

"Someone with your frame should not be so silent," she whispered.

"I am a hunter," he replied, as if that was enough.

Helesys frowned and stooped to the dirt. The cylinder was filled with concentric rings spaced two fingers apart and each wrapped all the way around the space. The spacing was *nearly* perfect.

"What do you make of this?" she asked.

"Wormsign. Borehole." Taunauk emphasized the direction with his free hand. "Old passage," he repeated. He started across the borehole toward the other stone hallway.

Helesys shuddered. It wasn't that the borehole was from a worm or any such factor, it was merely from the size. They were amnesiacs in a strange place and the first sign of other life was a giant beast. It did not bode well.

She flexed the mechanical fingers of her wand-arm, feeling the power course within her and most of the foreboding feeling left her.

But not all.

~

They went across and climbed up to the next stone hallway. Taunauk led and Helesys followed. The eerie silence stretched on just as the hallway did and Helesys's mind insisted on filling it...

Again, thoughts drifted to her wand-arm and the kindled power that lay within, comforting like a campfire. Helesys knew of magic—knew that weavers twisted the latent energies of the world, harnessed them, channeled them—and that she was one of those wielders of magic. ...But so much was lost.

She could think of no spells that she knew—no spells at all. Her memory loss had taken not just memories of home, but memories of how to create and destroy.

She could only hope that bits would come back to her or that she would remember them innately. So as she walked behind the barbarian down into depths unknown, she flexed the mechanics of her arm trying to will some bits of knowledge from them. But none came from such gentle teasings.

Water sloshed beneath Taunauk's feet. It was the first sound she'd heard from the man—she'd nearly forgotten he was there.

Puddles littered the hallway. Eventually the hallway was completely flooded and water sloshed with each and every step.

Taunauk grunted in disapproval.

"What's the matter?" Helesys whispered. She pictured him as a big cat who didn't want to get wet.

"Hard to be quiet. Going to get deeper."

Helesys was about to ask what the barbarian meant when she realized that the hallway was on a slight decline. They were walking deeper underground, which gave the illusion that the water level was rising.

An hour later and the water was shin-deep and sinking into Helesys's boots—frigid—and the elf gasped quietly as it filled her shoes.

Taunauk must have heard because he said, "I will not carry you."

"You will never need to," she replied through gritted teeth.

Soon the water was up to her knees, but mercifully leveled off.

In the distance there were pinpricks of light. Taunauk quenched his torch in the water and set it against the wall. Again the barbarian moved in a crouch. This time even slower than before so as not to slosh water and give away their approach.

"Do you think it wise to sneak up on our first contact?" Helesys whispered.

Taunauk stalked forward without replying.

The minutes drew tense as they approached and then the stone hallway opened up again. The pair stopped at the threshold. A sprawling, flooded room lay before them.

The flooded room extended back at least one hundred paces. At first, it wasn't readily apparent if the water deepened or not, but Helesys focused on the torches and the figures in the center. Four vaguely-Terran shapes huddled beneath the torches. The crouching posture gave the impression that the water was still shallow in the middle of the room. But as the elf looked closer she realized the figures were anything but Terran.

The four creatures had the figures of short, squat men but with huge heads and wide eyes. Great whiskers extended off of their faces and out past their shoulders. Their skin was sleek and shiny, and rippled with scales. One of the four towered over the others, but was still no taller than Helesys. Each seemed to hold a spear and a shield, save for the large one which held only a curved staff.

"Fishmen," Taunauk whispered. "Not good."

The creatures took turns tearing at a carcass that lay on its side and part of the side and a large fin stuck out of the water. One at a time they would duck down and viscous sounds would echo over the water. Then they would come back up, gnashing great chunks of red meat between spiked teeth, the white of which glinted in the torchlight.

The large fishman did not eat, but seemed to be gnashing its teeth incessantly, punctuating with a gesture of the curved staff. The manner looked vaguely ceremonial to Helesys.

The elf looked over the room: The opposite side, past the fishmen, looked to be nothing more than blank stone.

To the left, the room rose up a slope of jumbled stone and rubble as if the entire side had partially collapsed. The slope rose all the way up three or four stories to the stone ceiling of the room. It was completely exposed and offered no path forward through the dungeon.

To the right, a jumbled mass of twisted, rusted metal that spanned the entire side of the room. Though the structure had long-since been compromised, grid-like spacing was still intact behind the twisted mass of bars. It looked to Helesys like the mass had once been part of a prison, long since ruined and abandoned. The rusted prison could be laden with passages, but it was impossible to say from afar and they would need to pass the fishmen to get there. Swimming in the shallow water was out of the question.

The two scanned the slope and the rusted prison until they were satisfied that no movement came from either side.

The only way across was past the fishmen to the rusted prison and Helesys shared her ally's instinctual sentiments about the creatures.

"I'll follow your lead," she whispered.

The water rippled only once and Taunauk stalked forward with eerie silence, Helesys to the right and behind him. Tension overcame her as the pair descended upon the oblivious fishmen, like some great boulder at the start of an avalanche.

Helesys's heart beat faster and she forced herself to breath steady and slow in spite of it. The arcane gears and pistons in her arm hummed with menacing purpose.

Across the way, the fishmen continued ravaging the shark corpse, naive to the danger approaching just past the reach of their torch-light.

Fifty paces away in the gloom… Then forty…

The pair were thirty paces away when the largest of the fishmen ceased its incoherent chanting and turned their direction, torch-light glinting in its large eyes. Its mouth opened in a hiss that echoed through the flooded room. The three other fishmen raised shields and spears.

But Taunauk was already upon them.

He met the hiss of the fishman with a growl of his own. The barbarian pounced like a jungle cat—from standing still to his entire body soaring out over the water. He flew with axe raised overhead and came crashing down upon the closest fishman. In a splash of water and a screech of metal he brought the head of the battleaxe down through the creature and cleaved it in two.

It was an incredible display of athleticism, except that now Taunauk's massive frame and splashing was blocking any hope Helesys had of a ranged attack. She felt the magic spinning up in her arm like a windmill in a stormgust. She *knew* that all she had to do was level her hand at the creatures and a torrent of horrible violence would spring forth—yet she also had the feeling in her gut that Taunauk might get caught in the blast.

"You thundering oaf," Helesys mumbled. She waded further out to the right, hoping that she could get a better angle.

Meanwhile, the barbarian swung in massive arcs, the axe-head screeching as it deflected off the shields. The big fishman had stepped back from the fray and was hissing rhythmically and gesturing with its staff. Helesys recognized the casting of a spell, though she couldn't understand nor fathom which one it might be. In spite of that, there was one reliable way to break a weaver's spell.

Helesys raised her arm, palm out and fingers spread—trusting that she would know what to do in spite of her amnesia. Purple electricity crackled between her fingertips and she felt the machinations within the arm align, channeling the magic of the wand. Something akin to purple lightning erupted from her palm in a thunderclap that overshadowed all other violence.

The sound and the force surprised her, made her wince and spin. Helesys saw just enough as she lost balance and fell back into the water—enough to see the big fishman's torso split in two.

The elf gasped and tasted brine as she sprawled into the cold water. She struggled, slipping on the stone bottom and finally got her arms under her. She felt ridges—rope—and as Helesys finally broke the surface to breathe, something pulled at her feet. A rope net, concealed below, sprung up and over her head. Gears whirred and clanked off to the right where the rusted prison lay, and the rope net yanked her off her feet, down into the water again as she was pulled through the water.

Helesys twisted in the shallow water as she was dragged. She managed to rise above the surface for only a moment— enough to grab a half breath—before plunging under and tumbling along the bottom again.

Then there was a metallic snap and she felt the surge stop. The rope slackened as she floated to a stop. The elf weaver managed to half-stand, still trapped, and saw that she had not been pulled all the way to the rusted prison. She didn't pause to contemplate whether the trap mechanism had failed. She fumbled her left hand—her true hand—for a small knife on her hip, hidden in her robe.

And as Helesys slipped the knife and set to the rope net, she looked to Taunauk's brawl, but saw only the fishman that had broken off to avenge its fallen leader—the fishman swimming in a fury toward her. Its wake splashed and broke wide, blotting out everything behind it. It screeched mad and drowned out everything else.

The elf envisioned the brave Taunauk overcome at her moments tumbling underwater—the fishmen having slain him or left him wounded in the shallows. She envisioned that behind this screeching fishman was his brethren, come to tear her apart.

Helesys raised her gauntlet and felt the arcane violence churn again. She screamed and the fishman was nearly close enough to touch before a massive axehead descended like a starfall and cleaved the screaming creature in two. The shallow water split and exploded like a blastshell had been dropped.

And when the roar of the splash settled, Taunauk stood over her, staring at the crackling energy at her fingertips.

The elf lowered her weapon and cut thrice more at the net to free herself. She stepped out and pushed the net away in the shallow water. Meanwhile the barbarian stared at her wand-arm.

"Clever sheath for a wand," Taunauk said and gestured to the metal arm. "Elven?"

"I do not know," Helesys replied, turning her hand over. It looked or was made to look like a sleek gauntlet—it was anything but.

"Do you remember your teachings?"

The elf shook her head again. "I called upon the magic of the wand with merely a thought… I do not know what else it can do."

Taunauk nodded. "The memory lies somewhere within you. I could not remember battle, yet the weight of my axe is familiar."

"An echo," Helesys said, recalling the barbarian's comment in the first room.

Taunauk half-smiled in the gloom and gestured for her to walk with him. She wondered if that was the extent of the outlander's expression.

~

The two waded through the knee deep water of the flooded room with less worry and passed the carnage of their battle. The smell of oil and fish was heavy in the still air. Pockets of deep red blood mixed with the still-bobbing water. The fishmen seemed more numerous than before, but Helesys suspected that was from their being cleaved in two—by Taunauk's axe and by her magic cannon.

But the numbers did not match: There was one that nearly came upon her in the net-trap. The first that Taunauk had killed in a single leaping blow and the fishman-weaver who Helesys had blown apart with magic.

"There should be one more body," she said.

"It swam away. Down the well," Taunauk pointed out a ways toward the corner of the room where the water turned a deep, dark blue. Who knew where the underwater passage led.

"Will it return?"

Taunauk grunted, "Not for a time. Fishman was smart to run. May muster allies and return, but not for a time."

"Then we will be long gone," Helesys replied.

She was ready to be away from there and back in a dry passage. Now that the excitement of battle was over, the cold was returning. The water was not icy—not deathly cold—yet she knew that prolonged exposure would sap her strength. Strength she would need for whatever else lay ahead in this cursed place.

Taunauk grabbed the torch that lay propped on the body of a fishman; the single torch that stayed lit. They searched the flooded room. Both scanned around and below the waterline, weary for anymore traps that might be waiting for a wrong step. When they were sure there was no other way forward, the two waded toward the rusted prison.

"I did not expect anything to escape your axe," Helesys said in a quiet attempt at conversation.

"The two split. One for you and the other for the well."

"Ah, so you diverted to help me?"

Taunauk grunted in affirmation, then shrugged. "I see now that you needed no aid."

Helesys smiled. "I am not so proud as to turn my nose up at help."

They were nearly at the hallway when the barbarian paused as if gripped by a thought.

"We must relearn strategy," he said.

She raised an eyebrow at the giant human. "Do you think we used to know each other?"

Taunauk stared at her, his eyes hidden in the dim. "This life echoes. I feel it with you as well."

Helesys stared back. She could not say for sure that the barbarian was wrong. There were things she knew inherently. She felt her wand-arm and managed to call upon it. She knew of the hidden knife on her hip. But she did not feel the same about him. She did not feel him as an enemy, ally, lover, friend or kin.

She hoped that it was merely her muscles remembering a little quicker than her other faculties.

Taunauk must have sensed her lack of commitment. "It is no matter," he added, turning toward the hallway. "I trust that all things will come back to us in time."

"What about strategy?" Helesys asked. "I feared I would catch you in the blast."

"Good eye for the weaver," he said, ignoring her concern. "His chant was a hex upon my axe. They would have died more swiftly."

"Then I will target weavers and archers," Helesys said. "What will you do?"

"I will go first. And I will give your magic a wide berth."

~ ~ ~

The Rusted Prison

The first floor of the twisted structure was almost completely collapsed, no higher than the knee-deep water of the cavern. The fishmen could possess a passage beneath it, but none befitting an elf and a human.

They had to climb to reach a passable level of the twisted structure. Taunauk went first, he stowed the torch in a sling on his back where it rested along the massive battleaxe. He climbed methodically, testing handholds and footholds, casting strange shadows on the twisted metal. The prison groaned at the intrusion. The second floor was covered with barred doors and Taunauk paused, perhaps contemplating forcing the door aside, but continued up.

Meanwhile, Helesys mentally marked his path. If the bars could hold his weight they would surely hold her.

Taunauk scanned the third, but ceased his climb on the fourth floor and stepped off onto a landing. For the briefest moment the barbarian disappeared. Even his torchlight.

But the briefest moments can stretch on and in the gloom and in the cold of the dungeon, Helesys felt utterly and completely alone. Company was a comfort that she might not always possess.

Torchlight returned and though it was four stories up, it brought the elf a little kindling of warmth. Taunauk leaned over the landing and beckoned her up with a wave.

Helesys climbed the rusted prison, the gnarled metal groaning much less than before, but still protesting her ascent. Though she was set to task, her mind wandered, puzzling over how the body and even the mind could know things innately as they did: Commanding her metal arm with a thought, fear of prolonged exposure to the cold water, fear of the fishmen, the feel of blastshells exploding, Taunauk remembering the feel of his axe…

Perhaps some things were merely instinctual or ingrained so deeply they were indiscernible. Had the swing of an axe or the call of a wand become akin to walking or breathing? Taunauk knew he was a hunter, without remembering the specifics of his life…

But Helesys did not know what she was—a weaver, yes—but it seemed like a tip of the truth rather than the whole of the spear. Perhaps both she and Taunauk would live long enough to remember their lives and their truths.

Helesys easily followed the barbarian's path up the twisted bars. When she was within arm's reach, Taunauk offered her a hand and pulled her up the rest of the way as if she weighed nothing at all.

Past him, torchlight stretched down the orange-red hall. The walls were a mix of crumpled paneling and bars, not a single one spared from rust and decay. Swirls of rust-dust lined the floor, punctuated by Taunauk's giant bootsteps.

"There appears to be a path," the barbarian said, gesturing with the torch.

She stared and finally saw: The rust-dust seemed to flow in a pattern down the hallway, like river silt marking the twists and turns of flow.

"No fresh tracks," he added.

"No fresh tracks *here*," the weaver corrected.

Taunauk grunted in reply. "Keep your eyes open."

~

Helesys decided that she did not like the rusted prison, even more so than the cold, flooded passageways.

For one, the glow of the torchlight was both necessary and damning. There were no torches in the rusted prison—no other sources of light at all—and so without the torch they would've been nearly blind. But with the torch they were a beacon to any creatures within and also nearly blind to anything beyond their path, for the light of the torch cast uncountable shadows against the rows of bars, obscuring everything beyond.

And it was impossible to be quiet. Even as the elf tried to time her steps so they fell with Taunauk's, their weight betrayed them. Every minute or so, the floor beneath them would groan, as if calling out to any denizens that there were intruders within the walls.

But none came—not until the floor shifted beneath their feet.

A clang of metal beneath their feet that echoed through the entire prison. Both the elf and the human froze, afraid to move.

And from the dappled gloom of the rusted hall, a black form floated toward them. It was nearly as wide as the hallway and as it came closer, Helesys saw the outline of an ink-black squid. Its dozen arms pulsed, thin black skin covering and stretching between them. It floated slowly, steadily toward them like a specter.

Taunauk raised his axe.

"Do not do it," a voice hissed from their left.

Helesys turned, readying her wand-arm and at first she saw nothing behind the cursed forest of shadows. It was only when she heard the voice again that she saw a hint of the creature.

"The empty cell beside you. Hide there. Be quick." The voice came from behind a dozen shadows—sinister threads of fangs and a single massive, yellow eye.

Taunauk stepped carefully into the cell beside them, but he had not taken his eyes off the approaching squid. He had not seen the sinister look of their savior. Reluctantly, the elf followed.

Both watched the silent procession of the squid—eerie and eyeless—bobbing slightly with each pulse of its limbs. It stopped right in front of their cell. Right where the floor had creaked beneath their feet. Hunting by sound.

In the dappled shadows, Helesys saw more movement from their savior's direction. Accompanied by the faintest patter of feet. So faint that the squid did not bother with it. Helesys held her breath so she could follow the sound—back the way they had come.

Then another clang came from that direction, sharp and purposeful. The squid followed the new sound. For some reason, their hellish-looking savior was leading the creature away.

Neither Helesys nor Taunauk moved while the squid floated down the hall.

Then they heard an ear-piercing scream, short and violent. A shriek that echoed through the rusted prison a dozen times over. Deep in the depths of shadow the entire prison began to writhe. Shadows of squid began to float all over.

A procession came. A dozen squid floated by. Beyond, it seemed as if the entire prison was writhing as tentacles danced in the shadows. All converging on the source of the sound.

And when the last squid floated by, Taunauk stalked out of the room, leading her further down the hall, away from the creatures. Helesys looked back for only a moment and saw the black mass congregating in the distance. An uncountable number of squid pooled there—flooding the hall.

~

They didn't stop for several minutes, and moved at an almost reckless pace through the rusted prison. They only stopped when they heard the scurrying of feet behind them, then through the prison cells around them—their gruesome-looking savior—moving with animal-like deftness through the thin, twisted confines.

The massive, yellow eye, the width of two hands, stared back at them from beyond the bars two rows away. The black pupil shrunk to a pinhole as Taunauk raised the torch against the bars. Its skin was reptilian and spined at the joints, caked with rust-powder. Its limbs were abnormally long and thin, folded as it crouched low, yet it could reach up and grasp bars along the ceiling.

It flicked long, clawed fingers against the metal and hissed, "Avert the light."

The barbarian grunted and palmed both the torch and his axe in one hand, such that the head of the axe blocked the light of the torch.

It approached with rodent-like dexterity, slipping through narrow gaps in the bars. It chattered its needle-thin teeth as it neared the final set of bars. The pupil of its puss-yellow eye half-filling it.

Helesys's wand-arm whirred with steady power, elbow half-bent in anticipation.

"No closer, creature," Taunauk said.

"You should thank me," the creature said, its eye flitting between the two. A strip of black flesh hung from its mouth.

After a long moment, the elf replied, "Thank you for your diversion, but no closer."

"Ah, you're welcome, weaver." Its words lingered in a hiss.

"Why did you help us?" she asked.

Its eye flitted back to the elf, moving rapidly down and up, lingering long on her right hand. It grasped the rusted bars that separated them, its fingers alone were over a foot long—it would've been nothing for the creature to stick its arm between the bars and reach her.

Helesys called upon her wand and felt arcane energy crackled between her fingertips. The creature's dagger mouth opened and its pupil widened, nearly blotting out the yellow.

"Answer me," she commanded, "and be careful your hand does not get you into trouble."

Its fingers wrapped around the rusted bar. "I've never seen such a contraption." Its words were a gentle hiss now as it was transfixed on her metal hand.

"You are a weaver?" she asked.

"Yes—no… I was. We were all many things, once."

"Before this rusted prison? Or before the dungeon?"

The great yellow eye looked away from her wand-arm for the first time when she mentioned the dungeon. It stared at her for a long moment without speaking.

"This creature is of no help to us," Taunauk said. "It is a hoarder. A seeker of treasure."

"Shut your mouth, outlander," the creature replied, lowering its gaze to the floor. "I have no business with those who commune with the dirt and with trees."

"Then speak your peace quickly," the barbarian grunted, the wooden torch creaking under his grip.

"What is your name?" Helesys asked.

The creature looked at her with its wide yellow eye. "My name was Lull."

"Then Lull, we are leaving this place. The rusted prison and this dungeon soon after…"

Helesys had meant to continue the statement, but the creature's mouth opened wide and curved into a smile filled with hundreds of crooked needle-thin teeth.

"What is the matter?" she asked, metal fingers bristling in anticipation.

"You will try to leave. You may even make it far, but you will find no exit. No means of escape—"

"I've heard enough of this," Taunauk said. "I am leaving."

Taunauk's weight shifted and the rusted floor creaked ever so slightly. Lull's fingers rose and fell upon the bar. "I will see you again," it said. Then it reached out slowly for Helesys, reaching toward her right arm. It would be an easy thing for Lull to grab her.

Helesys's wand-arm whirred to life as the thin, gnarled fingers grew close, as if it sensed the approaching danger. It would be an easy thing to destroy the creature. A single blast had decimated the fishman-weaver. One this close would leave nothing left of pitiful Lull.

The elf whispered, "Don't make me—"

—Lull gasped as light spilled across the twisted hall. Taunauk had uncovered the torch and waved it near the bars. Scattered light fell across the thin, scaly demon.

"Be gone, creature. Trouble us no more," the barbarian growled.

In a moment, Lull had scurried another row away and whispered, "Sometimes I'm here… Sometimes I'm somewhere else. But you will see me again." The single yellow eye blinked and was gone. Lull's scurrying footsteps disappeared across the rusted prison.

~

Minutes passed with nothing but the occasional groan of the prison beneath their feet. Helesys continued looking back over her shoulder and even holding her breath until she was absolutely sure they weren't being followed.

Soft green light began to break through the prison. Helesys thought that maybe—somehow—they had reached the surface. That moonlight was washing through the twisted metal, giving it an underwater glow.

Instead she found moss.

Gently glowing moss-lined stretches of the walls and bars, muting and drowning out the orange rust that she had grown accustomed to. It would have been beautiful, except that now she was overcome by stillness. Without the threat of Lull or the floating squids, the prison was utterly empty.

Helesys found herself desperate to fill the void. "You didn't have to be so short with Lull."

Taunauk sighed. "That creature is not to be trusted."

"That was plain to see, but we could have gotten information from it."

"Twisted words from a twisted creature."

"My point still stands," the weaver replied.

"Animals do not think like us. It is a mistake to think so. Deadly mistake."

"Did Lull seem like an animal to you?"

"...No."

"Nor to I," Helesys replied. "*It* seemed like a Terran or a twisted version of one."

"It is no matter."

"Of course it is. If Lull is really a Terran, then it could be of help to us. Perhaps it could tell us about this blasted place."

"It is not to be trusted," the barbarian repeated. "The most dangerous creatures are the ones that can talk."

"What about those that refuse to talk?"

Taunauk grunted in reply and Helesys abandoned the conversation. How had two as different as they wound up in this cursed dungeon? Would their differences only grow as their memories came back? It was a pointless line of questioning, yet in the twilight glow she entertained it.

She had a feeling they were both right in their own way: They could not go around blindly killing any and everything they came into contact with. Yet Lull had reached for her gauntlet; that could not be denied. The creature had known something about the true nature of her arm, even before she activated it.

If the creature was right and they did see it again—perhaps if they were forced to double back—then Helesys would not let her guard down. But she would also try to get every bit of information out of the pitiful Lull that she could.

~

The faint sound of their bootsteps on rusted metal was overshadowed by sounds of water and screeching. They saw faint torchlight through the twisted cages—fixed and unmoving—and for the first time, Helesys found herself wary of the light.

The rows of cages of the rusted prison became intermittent. Larger. Helesys looked upon the new rows with wonder. Some were twice the height of Taunauk, then three times. The further they walked the larger they grew, the less rust appeared on their surfaces and the less mangled the bars were.

Helesys wondered if any of these new cells were in use. The elf did not have to wonder long.

In the gloom of the torchlight, a serpent-like creature paced idly in a three-wide cell. It coiled around on itself, for even in the large cell the creature was as wide around as a man and thrice as long. Five pairs of legs lined its middle and marched in unison. The beast was covered in scales of a deep purple that seemed to shimmer in the gloom. The serpent's head was both short snouted and tall, and it had two pairs of red eyes. One pair to the front and one pair high on the back of the head.

Though the serpent was clearly confined, they had no desire to pass close to it and risk calling another mass of blind-squid—or worse—upon their position. After a minute of searching, Helesys found another passageway through some of the last Terran-sized cells.

This time, a small cell was occupied with a gaunt-looking fishman. It was huddled in the back corner of the cell, limbs wrapped around itself. Its scales were dry and cracked, oozing black ichor. Its arms were pitifully thin compared to the fish-men the elf and human had fought before.

As they passed, the fishman's gaze followed them with half-closed eyes. Its mouth was still and closed, teeth hidden from view.

Helesys and Taunauk stopped near the bars of the cage and looked upon the fishman. "Do you think it is a punishment?" she whispered.

"No. Fishmen bleed red. It is diseased."

In the gloom of the torchlight, Helesys saw faint movement from other cells. At least half a dozen fishmen were kept in this portion of the prison, isolated and starving.

"It seems a cruelty."

"The fishmen are not stupid. There is a reason. Come."

That Helesys admitted. She pitied the dying fishmen for some reason that she could not say. It might have been because they were diseased or dying, or merely alone. The reason was as lost to her as the rest of her memories. Yet her pity was a small thing, a childish thing. Even she had some vague memory that diseases must be isolated.

As the elf and the human turned to leave, the fishman hissed. This hiss was weak and low, and rattled as if the creature's insides were shaking. Then the mouth of the diseased fishman opened—no, the face of the fishman opened—splitting in four as if an X had been cut into its face. The four corners peeled back, revealing a writhing flesh beneath.

The weak hiss grew only a little louder as the other diseased fishmen joined the horrid song, their voices rising in unison.

Something different than a simple disease festered within the bodies of the fishmen. Something that made Helesys step back. Her wand-arm hummed and her stomach dropped. Something unspeakable.

Helesys and Taunauk spared no more time for them and they did not speak of what they saw.

With any luck they would have found a way out of this hellish place by morning.

~ ~ ~

Ziggurat

They reached the end of the prison—or so they thought. The torchlight grew and only specks of rust remained. They had come to the final cage.

The bars of this cage were as wide as Taunauk and this single massive cell stretched from the cave floor to the full height of the cavern above. The cage was nearly the width of the rusted prison as well. It almost ran all the way to the cave wall on the right, leaving only small walkways between the cage and the cavern wall. Those thin platforms were the only way out of the prison.

In their traversing of the rusted prison and climbing up and down stairs, they had ended up on the third floor. They walked to the edge where the prison ended and the giant bars marked the last cage. Then they peered over and took in the sight. Enormous shackles sat on the cage floor, each one nearly the size of a single prison cell and must have weighed over one hundred stone.

Worse, the bottom of the cage was damp and smeared with shit.

Helesys looked further, past the final, giant cage out into the even more massive cavern beyond. The rusted prison sat at the top of a ziggurat—a stone-step pyramid. Helesys could just see some of the stones descending beyond the ledge. Past that, the sound of chattering filled the air—fishmen—the sound of dozens or even hundreds of them. Helesys imagined that the ziggurat's large stone steps were covered by fishmen.

Helesys and Taunauk ducked away from the edge of the overlook as two pairs of fishmen rose over the top of the zig-gurat and then approached that large cage. Each pair was pushing a great bulb of water that rolled and sloshed, like a giant, clear sack. These they pushed in a sweeping pattern, picking up the muck and grime from the cage floor. Behind them, a fishmen weaver chanted. It looked as if the weaver's spell was containing the water.

Meanwhile, the elf and the human waited patiently. They would not take a chance on the creaks and groans of the plat-form giving away their position.

Helesys's thoughts drifted back to the giant cage. What could the fishmen possibly be keeping in a cage that size? Something that was so very big and yet not tame? Taunauk was eyeing the cage too, measuring it, similar questions no doubt running through his mind.

When the fishmen left, rolling their sewage colored balls, the weaver and the barbarian stalked through the small plat-forms to the right of the giant cage. Here there were stairs leading down to lower levels and finally to the stone at the top of the pyramid.

Now that they were closer to the edge of the prison and closer to the edge of the ziggurat, the elf's fears were con-firmed. The chattering that filled the air was the sound of hundreds of fishmen. Each stone step of the ziggurat was as tall as a fishman and so they had covered many areas in animal hide, making primitive dwellings out of the corners of the stone steps. Fishmen covered nearly all the spaces between those dwellings. Some were hopping down the stairs, bearing shields and spears. The rest were gathered in great masses. These stood absolutely still while looking up at the cavern ceiling and chattering in unison.

There was no way they would get past that number of fishmen. The only spot that was bare was a wide stone ramp that led up to the massive cage.

The cave wall to the right, curved around and it seemed as if a stone path continued from the top of the ziggurat to some quiet safety opposite the fishmen. She pointed down through the bars to this right-branching path.

"That is preferable," the barbarian replied. So Taunauk led them down two flights of stairs to reach the bottom of the rusted prison—the top of the ziggurat. They paused at each level to be sure no more fishmen would return to finish their cleaning.

When they reached the stone, Taunauk said, "Wait here. I will go first. Look and return," and with that he moved quickly down the set. Again, surprising Helesys with his swiftness and quietness. The elf held her breath as he stalked toward the corner of the cavern, hugging the right-hand wall as he peeked around the corner. Then he disappeared around it.

Helesys's heart sped up as he crouched at the last stairwell. She glanced between the corner of stone and the edge of the stairs. Forty beats passed before Taunauk returned. He peeked around the stone and then stalked up the stairs as swiftly as he'd gone.

"There is a stone building with a door inside leading further. It appears empty of fishmen, but filled with faeries."

"Faeries?" Helesys cursed her amnesia.

The barbarian mimed a tiny creature sitting in the palm of his hand. "They are preferable to the fishmen."

The elf weaver shrugged. "We do not have much choice then."

"No."

Taunauk turned and surveyed the edge of the stone stairs before descending the metal ones again. This time Helesys followed, their bootsteps ringing quietly on the metal. They paused at the corner briefly and then continued around.

The stone building Taunauk spoke of was short and squat, taking up the whole of the passage—nothing but cliff to the right and stairs to the left. The building was cut into the face of the cavern such that only the face only stuck out an arm's length. The front of the building was shaped like that of a temple, with stone columns lining the front and a peaked roof. A small stream of water flowed out from the door and down the stone stairs.

The weaver and barbarian slipped inside and looked back. Thankfully their intrusion seemed to pass undetected.

~

Inside the short curved hallway, the single room of the stone building was a cross between a temple and an alchemist's laboratory. Huge stone statues flanked the entrance, abstract carvings of Terran species with clamshell faces—not fishmen, or human or elven. The statues and most of the room were covered in bright green moss, save for the clam-shell faces of the statues which appeared to be brushed clean.

Carvings decorated the corners, walls and floor of the room. The carved patterns were all curved parallel lines, giving the appearance of rippling waves all across the stone. The wavy carvings on the floor were cut deep enough that water followed them—steady water that came from under the door in the back of the room.

The door in the center depicted two more clam-faced Terrans kneeling with arms overhead in some form of prayer. Around the door were stone tubes that curved from all around the ceiling and congregated around the door. Water trickled from the bottom of these tubes, fed from somewhere high up in the cave.

All around, tiny blue figures of electricity danced through the air—faeries. Helesys marveled. Again, she knew instinctively that the faeries were not dangerous or devious. In fact, they brought a smile to her face—the opposite reaction she had to the fishmen. Helesys held out a hand—her left—for no other reason than she was curious, and was greeted by a single faerie landing on her palm.

The tiny creature was no more than half-a-hand tall. It too had the torso, head, and accompanying two arms and two legs of a Terran, but with two wings nearly the length of its body. The entire skin and wings were translucent and glowed a brilliant bright blue which spiked with white as tiny streaks of lightning bounced within it. It reminded her of the fishmen and their cleaning sacks of water, except that the faeries were barely-contained electricity.

The little faerie danced and twirled on the palm of her hand, folding its limbs and wings in an elastic manner before flying away.

Taunauk smirked and then turned his attention to the ornate door in front of them. "Ask the faeries how we pass through."

Helesys studied the little creatures. "It is an odd thing. With the fishmen I could not understand their language but *felt* the meaning of their chattering. I understand the creature, Lull, plainly.

"As did I. It spoke the common tongue."

"With the diseased fishmen and with the faeries, I do not understand them, nor sense their intent."

"Some creatures are far too strange. Does the moss speak with itself?" The barbarian nodded to the stone statues covered with it. "It must; it knows where to grow. Perhaps that is why the faces of the statues are not…"

Taunauk trailed off as a pair of faeries floated toward the face of a statue. They traced a circle with their tiny hands, one faerie starting from the top and the other from the bottom and flew around in a clockwise circle. They stayed perfectly opposite each other as they traced around the statue, their path steadily shrinking, steadily converging on the center of the statue's clam-face.

The whole display took little more than a minute and as the faeries traced their paths, Helesys saw the statue's face dull to a deep gray as the tiny creatures swept dissolved the faint green moss trying to get a hold on the claim-face.

And when the pair of glowing faeries reached the center their bodies burned white-hot and their spinning grew faster and then blurred together until two became one. Then in a brilliant, silent flash, the merged body split into three blue faeries.

Helesys and Taunauk watched, spellbound as the faeries joined their brethren floating around the stone room. The other faeries, if they perceived the event, reacted in no way to it.

"So much for your theory," the elf weaver jested.

"...The moss still speaks." He sighed as if weighing more words, then added, "Then we are on our own and must find a way through this door."

Helesys sensed there was more her comrade wanted to say, but stayed silent. The hulking warrior bent down and grabbed the bottom of the door and grunted in strain as he tried to lift the stone with nothing but brute force. The stone did not budge. He gave up after a few moments.

"There must be a way," he said.

Helesys turned her attention to the door as well. It was an intricate design and as she looked at it closer she realized it was a locking mechanism. There were a dozen pipes, but only some formed a path from the ceiling, around the door and ended at the floor—only these connected paths had water trickling through them. The other pipes were short, the longest no more than the length of a forearm and the majority only a hand-length.

If the pipes controlled the door then the different pieces could be moved. Helesys touched the stone, pushing and pull-ing—it only took a moment for a lone piece to spin. It was situated on a spinning plate which held four different pieces of piping. Though it took only a small force to find, it took both hands to spin the stone. As the plate and pieces spun, one of the flowing, completed lines was disconnected, and water dripped down the wall.

The elf weaver both ignored the dripping water and made a mental note of the original position, but continued spinning the plate. The next piece of stone piping did not connect properly, but the next piece did, redirecting the flow of wa-ter—yet still not making a complete path to the floor.

As she spun the stone plate, she heard the muffled clank of gears behind the wall. Helesys smiled. "Simple enough."

Taunauk grunted in affirmation. "I will watch the entrance."

She waved the barbarian away and looked over the rest of the piping—of the puzzle. She found five circles in all that changed the layout of the pipes and set to the task. It would be easy enough to simply try combinations until the correct one was achieved, but that would take time. Time they did not have. Who knew if the fishmen made routine rounds or if they would file in by the dozens to give thanks to these gods or ancestors. Helesys doubted they would be happy about their intrusion.

So she examined the wall further, listening to the clank of gears behind the wall. Then the stone door grumbled, but did not budge. She eyed the door curiously. "Taunauk, come try to lift this again."

The barbarian came over quickly and stooped down, again grunting in strain. This time they heard the dull scrapes of stone—of movement—but Taunauk could not do more than budge it. He groaned in frustration and stalked back over to the entrance.

Helesys spun the dials again, each time trying to turn them in such a way to make complete paths to the floor—since it seemed the gears only moved when paths were formed. Minutes passed as the elf tried combinations but none elicited that promising grumble of stone.

Something in the mechanisms was affecting the weight of the stone door.

"Quiet," the barbarian hissed.

The weaver turned and saw the faint movement of shadow in the hall. She ducked behind one of the two large statues that flanked the entrance. Footsteps. Then two fishmen warriors stepped into the room and stopped between the two statues.

They regarded the place with a quiet, tandem gnashing that re- minded Helesys of the cadence of prayer. After a moment they turned to leave. Neither the elf nor the human moved until they could no longer hear the footsteps.

Outside, the chattering of hundreds of fishmen was ever present. Helesys desperately wanted to get back to the trickling of water and the puzzle that might lead to their salvation.

"The mechanism," Taunauk whispered.

Helesys set to purpose and a thought occurred to her: If the mechanisms affected the weight of the stone door, then per- haps the flow of water was not the key. Perhaps the pattern of water was—the water in the pipes acting as a counterweight to the door. She would turn the plates and set the pipes to make the longest path possible, thinking that more water in the pipes at one time would lessen the weight of the door.

But as she set to the task, the fishmen returned—the elf weaver only knew because one cried out in a frothing scream. Helesys whirled around just in time to see the second fishmen round the corner and be cut in two by the massive battleaxe.

Outside, the faint chattering of fishmen stopped.

"We are out of time," Taunauk said. He stowed his axe on his backsling and crouched behind one of the large statues by the door. He roared in exertion and the statue toppled over, crashing horridly on the floor but blocking the lower half of the entrance. Taunauk ran and did the same with the second statue. This time it crashed on top of the first and though it leaned, it blocked the majority of the entryway.

The faeries whirled around Taunauk in impotent anger and he battered them away.

Helesys felt a pang of guilt, but turned back to the puzzle of the water pipes. There would be time later to beg forgiveness. If they survived. If she could even remember a god to atone to.

The elf's hands set upon the stone plates, looking for curves in the piping. The more curves she could piece together, the longer the piping, the more water would fill the piping and the more it would counterbalance the door. If her theory was correct. But it was not as simple a matter as she hoped, for the curves of one plate did not match the curves of another and so she could not simply turn the plates to the most curved positions.

"*Stercus,*" she mumbled in frustration. The slip was Elvish though the exact meaning escaped her.

Footsteps on the stone. Chattering in the entryway. The grunt of a barbarian. A dull chop and the scrape of axeblade on stone. Metal on metal. Helesys didn't dare look back, but she knew they were upon them, teeth gnashing in a frenzy of revenge.

The elf's mind raced, looking over the stone circles and the dozens—hundreds—of combinations. Only needing to be close enough that the barbarian's animal strength could take care of the rest.

She turned the stone circles one last time, satisfied with the positioning. She could no longer hear the dull clank of gears behind the wall over the ferocity swelling behind her, but she knew that this was one of the longest combinations of piping. It would have to do.

"Arrows!" Taunauk cried out.

Helesys dove to the right, half sprawling and half splashing across the floor. She heard the clinking of arrowheads hit the door where she had been standing.

She rose and hugged the wall to get to Taunauk. The toppled stone statues had not blocked the entryway perfectly and so fishmen were trying to clamber over and through an opening on the upper left. The little that Helesys could see beyond was filled with gnashing teeth and spears. The barbarian was chopping at anything that peered through, be it arm or head. Bodies were piling up in front of the opening as those in the back pushed their fellow fishmen through without patience or remorse. Taunauk alternated his assault on the opening with splitting injured fishmen that were pushed through and had fallen on the ground. Faeries clung to the upper corners of the room.

"Try the door, Taunauk," Helesys shouted over the fray. "I will cover you."

Her gauntlet whirred to life, the arcane mechanisms leeching power from the wand, burning with potential. The elf stepped out into the middle of the stone room and raised her wand-arm. Electricity crackled between her fingers and the purple arcane violence erupted.

The fishman crawling over the statue flashed with purple and exploded in chunks of scale and red. The blast passed through the entire hallway, and flashed purple and then red. The squelch of flesh being torn apart echoed through the stone hall and for a moment there was deathly silence. Helesys saw nothing but blood soaked stone through the opening.

A long scraping of stone behind her. She turned and saw the barbarian lifting the carved stone door. Taunauk strained, crouched and shouldered the stone door, finally standing all the way up with it.

Helesys needed no invitation.

As she ran to the door, she heard the gnashing of teeth and footsteps of dozens more fishmen pouring into the hallway.

Beyond that she heard the echoes of thunder and felt the stone beneath her feet shake—not thunder—something massive. Something the fishmen kept locked in the cage that stretched from the floor to ceiling of the rusted prison.

Helesys stopped just under the stone door. Taunauk breathed steadily, but clearly strained with the stone upon his shoulder.

"Be ready to drop the door," she told him. He nodded.

Helesys reached around the door to the stone discs and spun the closest plate with her metal hand, resetting the progress she had made. She heard the faint clank of gears inside the wall of the hallway. She spun a second.

"No more!" Taunauk grunted in protest. "I cannot—"

—Helesys commanded her gauntlet one last time to fire and a blast of magic shattered the plates and scorched the wall. With any luck it would stop their inhuman pursuers.

"Drop it," Helesys said as she retreated back into the hallway. The last thing she saw was the crazed teeth of the fishmen as they poured into the room.

Taunauk dropped the door and it crashed shut, leaving them in the dark.

~ ~ ~

The Drowned Temple

They had made it to the salvation of a short, dark hallway. The gnashing of the fishmen and the rumbling steps of whatever creature they commanded were muted behind tons of stone. The door had come down on the fringe of Helesys's robe, which she cut free with her knife.

Then the pair pressed forward, trying to put distance between themselves and the crazed fishmen. If there was any luck to be had in this blasted place, the fishmen would not be able to follow.

The short hallway was the same pitted stone and knee-deep gray water—but it was only short compared to the mile-long stretches they had passed through initially. Helesys followed just behind Taunauk and to his right side, giving her wand-arm a clean line-of-sight.

Meanwhile she kept glancing back the way they came, fearing that the fishmen would return in force. They were so far in the hall that the elf could no longer see the door from which they started. Even if they had a torch, the light would only reach so far. No screeches or splashing came from that direction—no sound at all—and she saw no silhouettes or bulging eyes across the water, yet her concern persisted.

Her gauntlet would be some help in the confined space, but there was no telling the limits of its energy… She doubted it would be enough to withstand the mass of fishmen they had seen on the stone steps.

Helesys pictured the violence again and the gruesome aftermath of her metal arm. It… It did not bother her much at all. She was an intruder here and in seeking asylum had very likely stumbled into a sacred place. The fishmen, gruesome as they looked, might have only been defending themselves and their home. Yet those facts did not give her pause, nor did the violence. The elf shuddered from the cold and not from anything else. That must have spoken to the Terran that she was before she lost her memory. …One numb to such violence.

~

Helesys and Taunauk left small ripples in their wake that traveled down the hallway and to the end of her vision in the gloom. She was never quite assuaged that those ripples at the edge of her vision were merely ripples of their passing and not something more sinister.

Blessedly, they were nearing the end.

From around the side of the barbarian, Helesys saw an end to the hallway and a soft glow beyond. Running water. Taunauk slowed to steady silence as they approached and she followed just behind.

At the mouth of the hallway they saw another room, this time gigantic and vaulted. Intermittent columns littered the room, supporting the massive spread. Each column was nearly ten paces in diameter—wider than Taunauk—and adorned with torches. The room sprawled out over one hundred yards to either side and even further directly across—so far that even with the intermittent torchlight it was hard to gauge the distance. The persistent flooding continued as far as Helesys could see.

The ceiling rose up and up, the full height of which she couldn't be sure of. The torches that lit the room only adorned the columns up thirty paces or so, giving the columns the illusion of rising up into an abyss.

All across the room, trickles of water dripped down from the ceiling and splashed into the knee-deep flooding. Were they not just underground but underwater as well?

"We found the source of the flooding," Helesys whispered. "Perilous place to build."

"Most strange—look." Something caught Taunauk's eye and he pointed out across the great room.

Helesys crept forward and saw in the distance a swirling waterspout—or so it seemed at first. It could only have been a little taller than Taunauk. Tiny compared to the massive room, but nearly as thick as the columns. As it passed from behind the pillars and back out into the open, the sound of running water grew louder. The pair watched the waterspout for several minutes as it wandered aimlessly around columns.

There was no wind. Not even a breeze. The air of the great room was eerily still.

Then the waterspout groaned and shook. At first Helesys thought the sound had come from the columns and had been caused by some unseen shifting of water above the ceiling but then it happened again and there was no mistaking the source.

The sound echoed through the cavern like the wooden groan of floorboards. Then twice the waterspout writhed with the sound, its swirling form pausing and becoming a silhouette of shoulders and a head.

A flash of light from its center—an object trapped within the creature.

Both realizations came suddenly, inherently: That the water phenomena was a living creature and that its soundings were cries of pain. Helesys knew not how she knew it, but the urge to help the creature welled up in her nonetheless.

She glanced to her massive companion. "Do you hear its pain?"

Taunauk nodded. "Do you know what the creature is?"

Helesys shook her head in frustration. "I do not, but it is clearly elemental in nature. ...I don't feel the same apprehension I did with the fishmen."

"Nor do I." The barbarian sighed, as if contemplating a plan. "Instinct can be powerful," he added, "But so can a creature in pain. Be weary of a wounded animal."

"I'll lead this time," Helesys said. "My magic will be more effective than your axe." The elf walked forward without giving him a chance to reply. She was a few steps out into the open air of the room before she looked back, just to be sure.

Taunauk was behind her. The nearby torchlight cast an enormous shadow behind him that made him appear to fill the room.

"I hope you're right," he whispered.

~

Helesys's heart was beating in her throat as they approached the water elemental. It spun and wandered the room, its path never certain and yet rhythmic, like it was following some incomprehensible waltz. Its sporadic wails echoed off of the stone and water.

Though the creature's shape was amorphous and swirling, the elf was able to predict its movements by watching the glint of the object embedded in the creature. She could see now that the shiny object in the center was a metal disc. Even more, in spite of the swirling body of water, the metal disk inside stayed still when the creature moved forward and turned only when the creature deviated its path. Helesys felt the metal disk was likely the source of its pain.

All the while, she had nearly forgotten about the cold that seeped into her legs and into her body—except for when she passed too close to a drizzle of water from the ceiling. The shock of cold water on her head and back made her wince.

When they were nearly in the center of the room, and only thirty paces away from the creature, Helesys paused behind a column to collect herself. She had no plan and no way of knowing how the elemental would react to her presence. It wasn't until she was nearly upon it that the realization dawned upon her that no fishmen were in *this* room—no creatures at all. Had they known the danger the wounded elemental posed?

The elven weaver steeled herself. They were too close and Helesys knew that she should help the creature.

"Stay behind me," Helesys whispered, "in case this goes to *stercus*." The curse felt versatile enough that the barbarian would understand her meaning. She walked cautiously up to the elemental, which had paused its waltz.

The arcane gears in her arm whirred to life, the energy of the wand within rippling with latent energy—Helesys ignored the weapon. With any luck she would not need it.

The water elemental sensed her approach. Its swirling form slowed as if the liquid was freezing solid and the metal disk in the center turned a quarter revolution.

Helesys stopped and was about ten paces from the creature, watching spellbound as its attention fell upon her. She had not forgotten about the familiar hum of power within her arm, but it did not bring the same comfort it had during her encounter with the fishmen. It would not be a decisive display of power, but perhaps it would be enough for her to survive to regret her decision.

The metal disk ceased turning, the swirling water of the elemental's body increased speed again—back to normal.

Helesys sensed the creature staring at her, though it had no eyes with which to do so. Then she heard its wail, like the sound of groaning floorboards. It resonated through the air and through the water, rippling its surface. The vibrations shook her lower legs—

—but this time she heard a gravelly, inhuman voice. The words sounded in her head rather than in her ears.

You are foolish.

"You are hurt," she replied.

A few seconds later the water rippled with the elemental's wail and Helesys heard the voice again in her head.

I am.

Then the disk within the creature turned and the elemental began to waltz away from her, but slow enough for her to walk beside it. Helesys kept the creature in the corner of her eye and followed.

Helesys sensed some small victory in speaking with the elemental, but now came the question of whether she could actually communicate with it.

"I see an object in your center. Is that the source of your pain?"

A long moment passed before the ripples came. *I think so.*

"I can help you. I can remove the object."

Will it hurt?

"It may, but then—"

—Helesys tripped over something in the water but caught her footing after a moment. She continued, "Then your pain will end."

You are foolish.

The elf nearly chuckled at the joke.

You are in danger.

She almost missed it over the elemental's constant cyclone of water. Behind her she heard a splash and then a groan. Something different, guttural.

Helesys spun, and saw an arm reaching for her—where she had just tripped. Putrid flesh, white tendon and bone beneath it. The hand reached for her as she recoiled, splashing after her. A Terran skull with thin wiry hair and red pockmarks just behind it. Gray-black void where eyes, nose, and tongue should be. A raspy breath in between each bite of its cracked teeth as the corpse crawled after her.

The cannon on her right arm whirred to life in some unspoken command. With a mind of its own, her arm reached out, palm nearly touching the gnashing face of the undead. Purple sparks danced across her fingertips.

Then came the jolt, but this time the elf was ready for it. The blast erupted from her hand and through the face of the corpse. The dull thump of impact mixed with a squash—the sound of bone and water pulverized—and then the water crashed back together. The motionless body, missing its head and shoulders, was hurled to the side by the waves.

But victory was short lived.

Splashes echoed throughout the cavern as dozens of undead rose up on rotting limbs. The closest were only a dozen paces away.

Behind her, Taunauk had already leapt and crashed down on one. Buying her time. His voice roared over the water and through the cavern, "Do not shoot! Do not hit the columns!"

"*Stercus*," she mumbled. The oaf was right—but that meant her plans changed only slightly.

Helesys turned to the water elemental. "Stop! Please let me help you."

The elemental stopped and then turned toward her, the disk in its center reflecting as it did. The creature said nothing until she reached forward with her metal arm.

Use your other limb, it said and recoiled from her touch.

So Helesys turned and reached into the waterspout, but in spite of the spin of the waves, she felt the water of its body was absolutely still. She plunged her arm in to the elbow, then the shoulder, but she still could not reach it!

Around her, corpses had risen and were stumbling toward her and the elemental on stuttering strides. Somewhere behind them axeswings crashed like blastshells, sending water and body parts flying through the air.

Helesys took a deep breath and reached even deeper, plunging her head and shoulders into the watery creature. This time her fingers found purchase around the disk and she yanked it free, stumbling out of the waterspout.

The elf found her footing just in time, just as the first three corpses set upon her.

Clutching the metal disk close to her chest, Helesys swung her metal hand toward the closest undead her fingers and palm crackled to life. A flash of purple, the dull thump of the blast and the squish of flesh and bone—the creature dropped, the lower half of its body slumping into the water.

The other two corpses stumbled toward her, gnarled fingers slashing in wide, gasping arcs. One lunged for her or tripped—she could not be sure—but Helesys ducked to the right, missing its grasp and keeping the fallen between her and its still standing comrade.

The elf raised her cannon arm and with unspoken command another blast obliterated the corpse that was still on its feet. The remaining half fell forward just as the fallen corpse was pushing itself up out of the water. Helesys called upon her arm again and caught bodies in the blast. The water in front of her exploded, sending waves and body parts flying across the torch-lit, flooded room.

Forty paces away, Taunauk fought with frenzied speed, continuing his plight to keep the bulk of the undead from reaching her and the elemental. Explosions of water littered the room, circling around the elf's position. The barbarian leapt and swung so fast—waves crashing and falling in constant overlap—that it felt like she was standing in the middle of a battlefield instead of an underground cavern.

Behind her, five corpses descended upon the water elemental. With breath in her throat, Helesys realized she could not help the creature. The waterspout was too large to shoot around and too large to circle around. Not before the undead reached it. She could only watch through the elemental's watery body as distorted shapes closed in.

But it needed no help. One by one, the undead reached for the elemental and were sucked in and then hurled into the nearby stone column. The action happened in the span of a gasp and with catapult force. In moments all five corpses were broken and floated like limp dolls in the water, skeletons shattered so completely.

Two more undead were upon Helesys and they met the same violent, splitting end at the palm of her cannon. Several more crunched against nearby stone at the surging of the elemental. All the while, the barbarian's axe crashed around them.

Violence filled the room and paused only once—when both weaver and barbarian scanned the room for any last corpses. There was only one and this time Taunauk marched toward it, his wake pushing aside the grisly remains that littered the water like stew.

Helesys turned back toward the waterspout. "Thank you."

The water around her rippled as the elemental replied.

Yes. ...The water is still and polluted. I cannot stay.

Even in the short aftermath, as the water elemental spoke, Helesys saw grisly chunks of flesh swirl in its body. A dozen questions bubbled up in the elf's mind, but one phrase spoke even louder within her:

"*Ut vos errare in aeternum et ut ubique esse domum tuam.*" Helesys said the old words because she felt she should. She felt them to be customary—necessary—and as she spoke them, she felt some magic flow with the blessing: *May you wander forever and may everywhere be your home.*

She did not know if the elemental would understand, but it replied in turn.

Yes.

The phrase was simple, but Helesys understood it to mean: *And the same to you.*

Then the waterspout shrank into the flooded room, its bright waters disappearing unceremoniously into the gray water of the flooded room. With waters that still churned with barely forgotten violence.

Then the water exploded with one last axeswing. With one last corpse.

~

Helesys turned to see her companion wading toward her from across the room. The full measure of the violence filled her sight. The entire breadth of the room was littered with the remnants of corpses. Had they slain so very many in such a short time?

As he approached, Taunauk's face came into view in the torchlight. A half-smile on his lips.

"I do not remember who I am, but gods that felt good," he said with a quiet sigh.

"We were clearly skirmishers," Helesys added. The barbarian's satisfaction spread to her, lifting her spirits.

"What of the disk?" he asked, nodding toward the metal clutched to her chest.

Helesys relaxed her grip—in the throes of battle she had nearly forgotten about it. She glanced at her wand-arm, realizing that she had thought only of it during the fray… It was such a powerful, yet innate, extension of her being that it had overshadowed her other limbs completely.

"What's the matter?"

Helesys pondered her gauntlet a moment longer before replying. "It is a small matter but… I feel as if I lost myself in battle. I thought only with my arm, or rather *did not* think at all."

Taunauk shrugged. "A tool is an extension of the body. A torch in the dark no different than an axe in battle. It is a piece of us. Does that trouble you?"

Helesys shook her head. Taunauk commanded his axe and the elf knew it would be the same if she held a torch. But her wand-arm felt like a mirror of that—as if it had thought for her, acted for her.

"I will dwell on it further," she replied, putting an end to the conversation.

The elf held out the metal disc and Taunauk stepped abreast with her so they could both examine it. It was an exquisite piece. Not a circle, but an octagon about the diameter of her hand and of the same thickness. The metal was sleek and shiny—whether this was in spite of the gray water or due to its entrapment in the clear waters of the elemental, she could not say.

One face of the disc was engraved with the shoulders and mane of a wolf. The design itself was a simplistic silhouette and yet exquisite in line and curve, as if it had been pressed instead of hand-made.

"What do you make of it?" Helesys asked.

"Stamped."

"I agree."

"Light enough to hold onto," the barbarian replied. "Do you feel magic within it?"

Helesys shook her head for she felt no magic in the plate. She turned it over in her hands, but could feel nothing that gave her that impression. On the backside, there were geometric ridges—purposeful, straight lines.

"Another stamp," she mumbled.

Taunauk grunted in affirmation. "No pattern. Strange."

"Purposeful," Helesys corrected. Made to fit somewhere…. "It is a key."

"Then we should hold onto it."

A screech split the quiet of the flooded room. Both turned to the far corner, to where the water deepened in hue. Another borehole and more fishmen with spears and shields raised. And in the center of the deepest blue, five sets of black eyes stared back. Each eye large enough that Helesys could see the thin vertical slit within.

The fishmen had found another way in.

The elf smoothly stowed the wolf crest in a front pocket of her robe and felt the churning of energy in her arm. Breath caught in her throat.

~

One by one, each of the five heads broke the surface: Massive, reptilian, each topping a coiled-muscle neck. Up they rose, taller than them, taller than the elemental, twisting around each other like great serpents rising nearly to the edge of the gloom

Helesys watched, spellbound, and vaguely aware that Taunauk was motionless beside her. The thought of dragons crossed her mind until the shoulders and body broke the surface and she saw that all five necks converged on the same massive frame. The body was nearly as wide as the spaces between columns. The forelegs even thicker than the necks above. The giant creature was covered in sleek, orange-gold scales that seemed to barely contain the knots of muscles beneath them.

She had seen the gargantuan cage and the chains. She had heard the thunder of its footsteps. But nothing could have prepared her for the overwhelming sight of it.

"By Movernus," she whispered, not knowing which god she invoked. A feeling of dread washed over the elf, one that overshadowed even the monstrosity writhing in front of them. She *knew* what the creature was but…

"*Hydra*," Taunauk sneered, giving a name to her dread. The five heads coiled and climbed over one another like snakes in a pit.

"We should run," Helesys whispered. "We—"

"We should," the barbarian said as he gripped his axe tight. "But we won't make it. Not knee-deep in water."

Helesys glanced at her comrade… She had seen the barbarian move and if he would not make it to the safety of the hallway then there was no way she would make it.

"*You* could make it," Helesys corrected.

"The fishmen aren't dumb—I will not die trapped in a hallway."

That was the other half of the elf's dread: The false-choice of escape. Even if they somehow outran the beast, certain death awaited them in the hallway. Taunauk was right.

Beside the five-headed reptile, a dozen fishmen chanted rhythmically and drew patterns in the air with their staffs. Though Helesys knew not the spell, she was sure that they were casting a spell and that they were chanting in unison.

Back in their first fight, one fishman had hexed the barbarian… What could a dozen do?

"I have a plan," the elf said. "The fishmen are controlling the hydra."

Helesys felt the churning of arcane torrent in her arm and prayed that the blast would stretch that far. Power churned. She raised her wand-arm—

—and with one decisive crash, the Hydra stepped to the side, shielding its masters from her sight. All five massive serpent heads ceased their twisting and stared at her with murderous purpose. Helesys, stared wide-eyed, directly at the beast.

"You are right," Taunauk said. "Separate. Try for the weavers and if we fail, blast the columns and bring this cursed place down upon their heads. It will happen fast—"

—The slits in its eyes widened and all five mouths opened, each with hundreds of spear-thin teeth. A cacophony rang out from the beast: Part hiss, shriek and bellow.

The Hydra thundered forward, covering ten paces with every step. The water around their knees quivered with each impact. In the span of the second it took three steps and was halfway to them.

The nearest column to the elf was a dozen steps away but it might as well have been a mile. The elf turned and dove for the column, splashing chest first into the icy water.

Thundersteps shook the ground as Helesys sprawled in the water and pressed her back to the column. A single massive jaw, big enough to swallow her whole, clamped down to her right. The force shocked her—a split second slower and it would have had her.

One of the far heads screamed, a barbarian roared, and the body of the Hydra turned again with quaking steps. Her chance! Helesys spun toward the fishmen and felt the arcane power churn.

Instead of the fishmen, she saw a slab of orange scale nearly as tall as she was—the tail of the beast swinging and pushing a wall of water with it that blotted out the torchlight. Helesys ducked toward the column for shelter, and while the tail only brushed by the stone, the wall of water smacked her with incredible force. The elf was set flying by the impact of the wave and for a moment the world went black and silent and cold.

Helesys struggled in the churning water—trying to find the stones as she surged with the wave. Finally she found her footing and stood. Now she was in the middle, a dozen paces from any column—any salvation.

Meanwhile the barbarian roared and the beast's thundersteps shook the stones beneath her feet. The Hydra was turned away from her, but still spinning. She watched each head descend out of view and heard each slap of teeth as each head in turn bit at her companion. Still the barbarian roared.

The Hydra spun in a ferocious display. The first of its heads turned toward her.

Helesys turned again toward the far corner, looking for the chanting fishmen. She could only see a few—two chanting—from where she was but she wouldn't have the time to move. Not knee-deep in sloshing water. Her cannon whirred to life, filling with potential.

Thunder was growing closer and the massive creature was growing quickly larger in the corner of her vision.

Would it be enough? Would two fishmen be enough to break the spell?

As doubt grew in her mind, power surged in her arm. The arcane torrent built and built, rising like a symphony until it was painful, until the hum of power shook her teeth and bones.

At the last moment, Helesys turned and saw the Hydra, so big it blotted out the room. Five open mouths descended upon her.

And she fired right at it.

~

The recoil of the blast sent Helesys sprawling backward, skipping like a stone across the flooded room and then under the water. She tumbled as a wave bowled her over again. She breathed brine and coughed, gagging on water. Desperate for air.

She slammed into a stone wall—*the* stone wall—clear across the room. Her ears rang, and her collarbone and neck screamed sharp pain. Somewhere she heard the dull screech of the Hydra, so powerful she felt it rippling through the water.

Helesys opened her eyes to see a frothing ocean, waves taller than she—so violent that bare stone opened up in between. In the center of it all the Hydra thrashed, pulses of blood gushed from the center head, which was split in two to midway down the neck and hanging limp in front of the beast.

She heard the muted roar of Taunauk—so faint in her ears compared to the ringing and the screech of the Hydra. The other reptilian heads turned and met the barbarian in a fury half-blocked from sight by the crashing waves.

Helesys braced herself as another wave crashed into her. She winced and struggled to keep her footing.

The ringing in her ears faded and for a moment the Hydra was overshadowed by a barbarian's rage. But Taunauk's roar was cut short. Across the room, Helesys saw one head of the great beast tilt back and swallow what she could only assume was her comrade.

"No!" she screamed. "Oh gods." Her heart sank so deeply that she thought it might drown in the waves.

The Hydra turned toward the elf again, but this time it didn't charge. This time the great serpent heads turned on the dead neck and bit at it, tearing away chunks of dead flesh. The other heads tore and swallowed, eating the wound. The Hydra's body was still as it set upon itself.

And when it was done, the serpent heads danced and twisted around each other again, around the fresh bleeding stump. Then the flesh of the stump started to pulse and then to grow.

Helesys had seen enough, she turned for the fishmen. Both fists shook with anger. She raised her cannon for the few that she could see, still incessantly chanting at the other end of the room. She fired, not caring about the columns or the river above the room.

Two blasts sounded from her hand and crashed into the stone beyond—both too high and too wide. The fishmen continued their chanting and ducked out of sight. Now she saw nothing but columns. She turned back and slumped against the wall. Her legs were numb from pain or exertion or both.

The Hydra's four heads stared at her as the fifth—and sixth grew—two heads sprouting through thin red skin. It was a slow process and Helesys was growing impatient.

Her wand-arm churned with power again and she let it build. This time the pain thrummed through her bones almost immediately. Apparently even the arcane materials had a limit, but still she let it build.

It wouldn't be enough to slay the Hydra outright, but it would be enough for her purposes.

Helesys leveled her cannon at the nearest column and smiled, for her blast might possibly catch several in a line. Then she fired. The blast erupted, shattering clean through the column. The crunch of stone sounded twice as the purple blast punched through both columns in a row.

There was a tearing sound as the ceiling split, like the world might've cracked in two. Then water hissed from above and the entire underground groaned, the sound drowning out even the scream of the Hydra. The ceiling buckled, freeing a mountain of stone and a river of water.

Numb pain filled Helesys and she slumped against the wall and into the water. In spite of it, she smiled with satisfaction. A comrade avenged and a swift death.

All things considered, could she ask for anything more?

~ ~ ~

The Room

The next thing Helesys knew was blackness. Silence.
Then she was falling.

It was long enough for her heart to rise into her throat and no longer than that. She landed on both feet and crouched into a roll automatically. Twice over and then sprawled out on the dusty stone floor. Her wand-arm hummed with power.

The elf pushed to her feet quickly because a short step away someone else fell to the ground. Taunauk hit the ground in a crouch, catching himself through sheer strength alone. Though the axe was on his back, he rose to a fighting stance. Fists were clenched, knuckles white.

Both of them were alive and standing in the same stone room as they did at the start. Sparse torchlight. Ancient stone. Underground with no discernible entrance or trap door.

Memory of the ceiling collapsing played across Helesys's mind as she looked up. Surely with the mountain of stone and the river above she had been crushed… Yet here she stood. She relaxed the coursing energy in her arm and realized that it was fresh—untaxed.

Neither the elf nor the human spoke. The room was still and quiet except for their quick breathing.

Then Taunauk walked softly over to the torches on the right wall, his footsteps overshadowed by Helesys's rising breath. He ran a hand over the sconces, looking them over and when he reached the end of the wall he turned to her.

"I tore one from the wall. There are none missing. No hole in the stone," the barbarian said. He walked back to her.

Helesys looked down at the bottom of her robe where she had cut it free from the stone door—it was unmarred. Not a stitch of fabric was torn. She had been renewed, body, metal, and cloth.

"What do you last remember?" she asked, already knowing the answer.

"The maw of the Hydra. Death. Blackness," Taunauk's reply was calm and measured. Forced.

"I saw you die…" Helesys trailed off, remembering the battle cry of her companion and how it was cut short at the moment of his death. It was a reprieve to see him. "I fared no better."

She felt the edge of metal against her stomach and pulled the wolf crest from the pocket of her gray robes. The metal glinted in the torchlight. It appeared to be the same eight sided disc with wolf silhouette, though the geometric designs on the back—the side they thought was a key—were too complex to say if they had changed.

"Do you think we were wrong about the relic?" Taunauk asked.

Helesys glanced from the relic around at the stone room that seemed so familiar and yet was not. The sconces were different… or reset, like pieces on a game board. But even that was not quite right because the wolf crest was still in their possession. She felt no magic from the relic or the stone around them, yet *they were alive*.

"I wish I could remember more," the elf finally said. "Magic, no matter the kind, works with rules. We must learn the rules of the dungeon and the rules that govern our rebirth if we hope to make it out." She slid the wolf crest back into the front of her robe.

The barbarian grunted in affirmation.

Dungeon... Why had that word come to mind?

Then he walked over to the line of sconces on the wall and tore one free with the same easy strength.

"What of the Hydra?" Taunauk asked.

"My blast only killed one head, but after your passing the head started to regrow. When one head dies, two more take its place. My next shot I aimed at the columns..."

Then Helesys realized why he was asking. It was not out of curiosity or comradery. If the dungeon had been reset like a gameboard or like the sconces on the wall then they would likely need to deal with the beast again.

There it was again... *Dungeon*—a place underground for keeping prisoners.

"It is no matter," he said, having seen her expression. "We will find a way past the beast or we will give the fishmen a wide berth."

Helesys nodded and added, "You go first."

The barbarian chuckled and loosened his grip on the battleaxe. The elf weaver followed just behind him.

But then Taunauk paused at the hallway and was still. She could not see anything past his massive frame and could not even see his head past the fur cloak on his shoulders.

She grew impatient. They had a long walk ahead of them and the unending chill of water—*that* she had not forgotten. She shuddered at the memory of the cold. But as the moment stretched on Helesys began to fear that he was caught in some magical trap.

"Taunauk," she whispered, afraid to move.

"You must see for yourself," he said and stepped to the right.

She hesitated, but told herself that if there was danger Taunauk would not move aside. In spite of the thought, Helesys's every muscle was tense as she moved forward in a crouch. She looked left down the hallway. It stretched impossibly far into the gloom again.

It was the same as before: A sharp left. Ten paces wide. Stone-lined. Impossibly long. No torch sconces. She thought again of the blasted flooding.

"I do not understand—"

—The elf weaver's breath caught in her throat as she turned back toward the barbarian, for on the right was another hallway where before there had been only one. Both equally long and dark.

Helesys dropped to a knee and glanced again down both paths. Had she really expected a second chance? Another chance to sneak past the fishmen and avoid the Hydra?

From behind her, Taunauk said, "I think we should go left again."

The weaver paused, trying to weigh two unweighable options. Worse—another thought scratched at mind her like a spider crawling in her hair: Death likely waited for them. Death and rebirth.

"Okay, Taunauk. Let us see just how much about this dungeon has changed."

~ ~ ~

NEXT TIME ON

*A BATTLEAXE AND
A METAL ARM*

Book 2:

KNEEL BEFORE ZHUG

Available May 2021

Spoiler–Free excerpt from *BAMA 2*

Sneaking through the hall of the barracks was painfully slow. A hundred paces after the last bunk room brought them to a hard corner as the hallway turned to the right. Taunauk carefully peered around the corner.

"There is another bend up ahead," he whispered, then gestured with his hand to make a Z-shape.

"Good place for an ambush," Helesys replied.

The barbarian shrugged. There was little choice in the matter. Trying to sneak back past the ninety sleeping goblins was likely more dangerous.

"I will go first," he said. "Wait here."

Helesys felt eyes over her shoulder again, something watching. Something there and yet invisible. Intangible. She looked back over her shoulder and up and, for a moment, thought she saw something standing above her. She blinked and the image was gone, and the elf questioned whether she had seen anything at all.

Helesys alternated between watching her partner stalk the hall, which might've been another hundred paces to the next bend, and keeping watch on the hall of sleeping goblins. Her heart was beating in her throat. The arcane hum of her gauntlet was a small comfort.

Taunauk was halfway down the hall when he stopped cold and stood straight. He stepped to his left, flush with the stone wall so that Helesys could see.

Six goblins stood at the far end. They were all the same small, hunched build, except that these goblins wore haphazard armor. Their shoulder pauldrons and leg grieves were oversized, like they had been made for a man—or stolen from one. Helesys's mind wandered back to the piles of broken armor and wondered how they had come to pass. The goblins also brandished swords and shields and those in the back held bows, already drawn.

Helesys and Taunauk had made no sounds and their whispers should not have alerted goblins hiding around a corner such as they. Somehow they had known. Somehow they had been watching the elf and the human.

To be continued May 2021

Thank you for Reading

I hope you enjoyed reading this story as much as I enjoyed writing it.

If you did, I would massively appreciate a short review on Amazon or your favorite book website. Reviews are crucial for any author, and a starred review or even just a line or two can make a huge difference.

It's especially true for the start of a series. Thanks and I hope you enjoy the next one!

<u>For a limited time</u>: Sign up for Sam's *Monthly Newsletter* and get Free Phone and Desktop Backgrounds featuring art from *A Battleaxe and a Metal Arm*! Go to SamuelFlemingBooks.com to sign up, get some free digital art, and keep up with publishing and sales alerts.

Looking for more Bite–Sized Fantasy?

You might like **Tales from Another World, Volume 1**. The first installment contains stories about an undead sorcerer, a druid grove under attack, strange mermaids, a possessed church, a witch sentenced to burn, and commoners caught in-between.

The compilation contains the following stories ranging from 1,000 word flash fiction to 5,000 word short stories:

1) The Final Ritual of Sircius Everdeath
2) Under the Waters of Digsonee Strait
3) On the Crimes of Hexing and Bewitchment
4) A Final Plea upon Still Waters
5) The Crypt of St. Lillian
6) The Blessing of the Autumn Herald
7) City of Embers

What to expect in *Battleaxe and a Metal Arm*

I usually save this space for an "On Writing the story" section, but let's do things differently this time. So, what can you expect from this series?

1) You can expect a heaping dose of action, both of the battleaxe and magical prosthetic arm variety.
2) Expect to slowly learn more about Helesys and Taunauk as their memories come back.
3) Expect to learn more about the dungeon as our heroes explore its far reaches.
4) Lastly, you can expect a new story in the series every month. *Sword and Sorcery on a Schedule.*

I thought about going for a story every 2-3 weeks, but I wouldn't be able to keep that pace. I'd rather be consistent.

If you're reading this then the next installment is probably up for preorder. Don't forget to check out if you're interested!

Connect with the Author

If you want to stay up to date on the latest about Samuel's publishing news and blog, check out his website and consider signing up for his monthly newsletter.

www.SamuelFlemingBooks.com

Samuel can also be found on Reddit, Goodreads and Facebook.

Samuel Fleming is a Science Fiction and Fantasy author.

He grew up in Maryland, spending most of his time swimming and writing. Swimming gave him a lot of time to daydream, so the two hobbies complemented each other well. Idle dray dreams turned into stories, some of which stuck with him for years. These days he swims a little less and writes a lot more.

He loves a good story no matter the medium: Books, TV, video games, comics, tabletop RPG's, or podcasts–most of which he attempts to share with his wife and three kids, and occasionally on his blog.